Emily got as close to the bars as she could and peered in, her eyes straining. As she watched, there was a small movement in the basket and she saw the tip of a tiny tail.

Alison slipped the door open and gestured for Emily, her mum and her granny to follow her in quietly. They tiptoed over to the basket. In it, trembling and looking up at them with wide, frightened eyes, was a tiny Dalmatian puppy!

"He's called Bailey," Alison whispered as she scooped up the quivering puppy and held him in her arms so that they could stroke him. His fur was white but looked pinkish in places where his skin showed through and his nose and ears were black. He was dotted with spots and splashes of black fur and he even had a few marks round his nose that looked like freckles! Emily stroked him really gently as he squirmed in Alison's arms, hiding his face under her elbow.

Have you read all these books in the
Battersea Dogs & Cats Home series?

BAILEY'S
story

By

Sarah Hawkins

RED FOX

BATTERSEA DOGS & CATS HOME: BAILEY'S STORY
A RED FOX BOOK 978 1 849 41125 7

First published in Great Britain by Red Fox,
an imprint of Random House Children's Books
A Random House Group Company

This edition published 2010

1 3 5 7 9 10 8 6 4 2

The Random House Group Limited supports the Forest Stewardship Council
(FSC), the leading international forest certification organization. All our titles
that are printed on Greenpeace-approved FSC-certified paper carry the FSC
logo. Our paper procurement policy can be found at
www.rbooks.co.uk/environment.

Mixed Sources
Product group from well-managed
forests and other controlled sources
www.fsc.org Cert no. TT-COC-2139
© 1996 Forest Stewardship Council
FSC

Set in 13/20 Stone Informal

Red Fox Books are published by Random House Children's Books,
61–63 Uxbridge Road, London W5 5SA

www.**kids**at**randomhouse**.co.uk
www.**rbooks**.co.uk

Addresses for companies within The Random House Group Limited
can be found at: www.randomhouse.co.uk/offices.htm

THE RANDOM HOUSE GROUP Limited Reg. No. 954009

A CIP catalogue record for this book is available from the British Library.

Printed and bound in Great Britain by
CPI Bookmarque, Croydon, CR0 4TD

Turn to page 93 for lots
of information on
Battersea Dogs & Cats Home,
plus some cool activities!

Meet the stars of the Battersea Dogs & Cats Home series to date . . .

Bailey

Misty

Chester

Rusty

Max

Daisy

Battersea Dogs
& Cats Home

Emily's cheeks were nearly purple by the time her mum noticed her in the rear-view mirror.

"What are you doing?" Mum asked, laughing.

Emily noisily let go of the breath she'd been holding. "You told me to stop wriggling and not to move a muscle!" she said crossly.

"I'll let you move your lungs," Mum replied with a smile. "Besides, if you faint before we get there then you won't be able to help me choose the puppy!"

"Muuummmm!" Emily wailed before turning to look at her granny. "You have to let me pick him – I visit you so much don't I, Granny, that he'll sort of be my puppy too!"

"Of course he will, love," Granny said seriously. "I'm going to need your help a lot – you'll have to walk him when my leg hurts, and run about with him if he wants to play when I'm tired. It's going to be brilliant for me to have some company now that I don't have Patches around any more, but a dog is a lot of work as well as a lot of fun, and I'll be relying on your help."

Just then they saw a sign for the Home – they were nearly there! The car had barely stopped in a nearby street before Emily had pulled off her seat belt and jumped out. They were going to find the perfect friend for Granny – she just knew it!

"Hello," Alison, one of the Battersea team greeted them as they went in. She led them through to reception and sat them down to talk about what kind of dog they wanted. Emily's mum explained that the dog was for Emily's Granny, Mrs Taylor, who had been quite lonely since her elderly cocker spaniel, Patches, had sadly died earlier in the year.

"Patches was Granny's friend for eleven years," Emily told Alison, "which made him seventy-seven in human years – almost as old as Granny!"

"Cheeky!" said Granny.

"We live right next door to my mum, so we're going to be helping out a lot," Mum said, "and Emily's volunteered to be chief walker and pooper-scooper!"

Emily pulled a face. "What kind of dogs are there here?" she asked Alison.

"Oh, all kinds!" Alison replied. "We look after anything that woofs! We'll definitely have the right one for you. It's very important to make sure the breed of dog you get suits your lifestyle. Some types of dog grow very big, and some need lots of exercise. It wouldn't be fair to keep a Great Dane in a flat, they'd bash about and break everything – it'd be like you trying to live in a rabbit hutch!"

Emily giggled at the thought of trying to squeeze in next to a surprised-looking bunny!

"If he's for you," Alison continued speaking to Granny, "I think you'll need an older dog, maybe one that will like peace and quiet and taking it a bit slowly."

"You don't know Granny!" said Emily. "She's always racing about. There's a lovely park near her house and she used to walk Patches there every day."

"It's true," Emily's mum agreed. "Even though her leg slows her down sometimes, she's still very sprightly. We call her Action Granny!"

Alison chuckled. "In that case, I think you should come and have a look at the lovely puppy we've just got in."

She led them
over to a kennel.
Emily looked
through the bars
eagerly, but she
couldn't see a
dog anywhere.
She looked at
Alison questioningly,
but before she could say anything, Alison
put her finger to her lips, and pointed to
the large basket in
the corner.

Emily got
as close to the
bars as she
could and
peered in,
her eyes
straining.

As she watched, there was a small movement in the basket and she saw the tip of a tiny tail.

Alison slipped the door open and gestured for Emily, her mum and her granny to follow her in quietly. They tiptoed over to the basket. In it, trembling and looking up at them with wide, frightened eyes, was a tiny Dalmatian puppy!

Granny's Surprise

"He's called Bailey," Alison whispered as she scooped up the quivering puppy and held him in her arms so that they could stroke him. His fur was white but looked pinkish in places where his skin showed through and his nose and ears were black. He was dotted with spots and splashes of black fur and he even had a few marks round his nose that looked like freckles!

Emily stroked him really gently as he squirmed in Alison's arms, hiding his face under her elbow.

"He's very timid," Alison explained as she handed him to Emily. "We're not sure what happened to him but he's very wary of strangers. He does get friendlier when he's used to you, but he'll need a lot of love and TLC before he learns to trust you. He'll need a quiet home and a lot of attention, but he'll probably be quite playful when he's settled in. I think you and your granny sound like the perfect people to look after him. What do you think?"

Emily and Granny looked down at the little ball of fluff in Alison's arms, and Granny traced one of his beautiful black spots with her finger. Bailey shrank from her touch at first, but as she stroked his head he gradually pushed up against her hand, as if he was enjoying the attention.

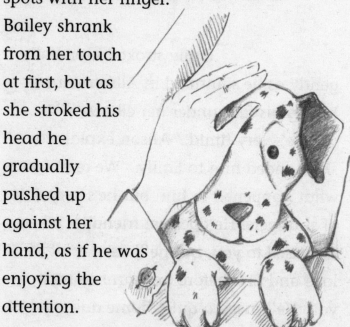

"I think he's beautiful," Emily breathed, her eyes shining. "He's just perfect for me." Mum gave a little cough and Emily giggled, "Oh!" she cried, "I meant Granny – he's perfect for Granny!"

"We know no one could replace Patches," Mum told Granny, giving her a little hug, "but we thought you needed a furry friend to keep you company, and Bailey really is the most beautiful little Dalmatian puppy and we'll all help look after him."

Granny gazed at them both with tears in her eyes "Oh, that's wonderful," she said as Emily's mum hugged her. "It'll be just lovely to have a dog in the house again!"

Two weeks later, after a member of the
Battersea Dogs & Cats Home team had
been round to check Granny's house was
suitable for little Bailey to live in, Granny,
Mum and Emily went shopping for the
new arrival.

Granny pushed the trolley while Mum
and Emily ran round the shop picking up
everything she needed. They bought lots
and lots of things for Bailey. The trolley
was piled up so high that Emily couldn't
even see Granny pushing it!

Emily raced about, trying to put things
in the trolley as quickly as possible, but
she got stuck when Granny asked her to
get a dog toy for Bailey. She just couldn't
decide which one she liked. There was a
nice red jangly ball or a lovely stripy
squeaky one. Or would Bailey like a chew
toy instead? Emily was standing in front

of the shelves for so long that Granny
came to find her.

"Hmmmm, this is a problem," Granny
said. "It's tough to know what Bailey
would like best. I think we're just going to
have to get all of them!"

Mum groaned when Emily and Granny came back to the heaving trolley with their arms full of toys. "Bailey is going to be spoiled rotten!" she said with a grin.

Granny had been determined to make
her cottage the best home possible for
Bailey, so she spent the next few days
furiously cleaning her already spick-and-
span cottage.

She even got Emily to help her move her
wardrobe so she could dust behind it!

Of course everything was fine, and the
Battersea lady had told Granny that her
little cottage and garden were going to
make a brilliant home for the puppy.

Settling In

The next day, Emily was walking home
from school with Mum. Well, she was
walking, jumping, hopping and skipping
about madly – because today was the day
that Bailey was coming to live next door
with Granny! Emily couldn't believe that
it had only been two weeks – it felt like
she'd been waiting for Bailey to arrive for
ever. Even the journey home from school

seemed to take much longer than
normal.

As they finally turned onto their road,
Emily dashed off, tearing straight up
Granny's path and bursting through the
front door.

"Is he here, Granny?" she
yelled as she raced in.

There was
a flash of white, and Granny tutted at
her excited granddaughter. "He *was*
here!" she laughed, "but you've scared
him and now he's hiding under the
table. He really is a very timid little thing.

Come and sit here
quietly with me
and he'll come
over when he's
ready. He's not
going to give
up his cosy spot
by the fire that
quickly!"

Emily poked her head under the
tablecloth and whispered, "Sorry for
scaring you,
Bailey." Then
she went and
curled up
next to
Granny and
told her all
about her day
at school.

She was explaining about a tricky move she'd made in gymnastics when Granny nudged her, and Emily turned to see a small black nose coming out from the edge of the tablecloth.

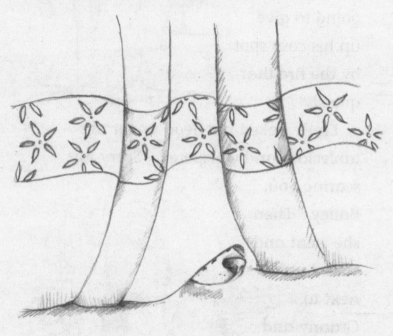

Granny reached for a dog biscuit and called him softly. "Bailey, come and see Emily. Come on . . ."

Bailey's nose twitched when he smelled the biscuit, and gradually he crept out from under the table. Emily gasped when he sneaked up close enough to take the biscuit from Granny's hand, and she slid onto the floor so she could stroke him while he ate it. Granny gave Emily a biscuit to feed him, and Bailey plonked his bum down next to her.

By the time Emily's mum called her home for dinner, Bailey was happily sitting on Emily's lap, still munching away.

"Can't I stay over tonight, Granny?" Emily pouted, "I want to stay with Bailey."

"Not tonight, dear," Granny said, giving her a

squeeze. "Your mum's cooked you a nice dinner and Bailey and I need to get settled in together. It's Saturday tomorrow and you can spend all the time you like with him. Come round in the morning and you can help me take him for his first walk, OK?"

"O-K," said Emily grumpily as she got up. Then her eyes brightened again. "But I get to hold his lead – deal?"

"Deal," said Granny with a chuckle, "Sleep well sweet pea."

The next morning was beautiful, crisp and sunny – a perfect winter day to go walking in the park. Emily grinned with excitement as she drew her curtains. Just then a movement caught her eye and she looked down into Granny's garden next door. Bailey was there looking up at her!

Emily threw open
the window and
waved at him.
"Morning,
Bailey!" she
yelled.

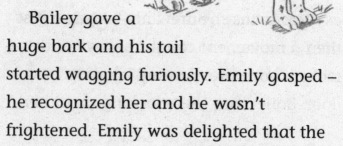

Bailey gave a
huge bark and his tail
started wagging furiously. Emily gasped –
he recognized her and he wasn't
frightened. Emily was delighted that the

timid little puppy was
already becoming
her friend.

Rushing down
the stairs, Emily
yanked open the
hall cupboard
and began pulling
things out of it.

She and Granny quite often took balls and rackets to the park to play with – and this time Bailey could join in!

"Gotcha!" Emily exclaimed as she found the rackets. Then she called out to Mum, "I'm going to Granny's."

"Not so fast, young lady," Mum called back, coming into the hallway. "You've still got your pyjamas on!"

Emily looked down at herself in amazement – she'd completely forgotten to get dressed! Emily's mum ushered her back upstairs and made her put on about fifty layers before she went round to Granny's. Emily grumped and stomped about impatiently as Mum laid out all her winter clothes, and even stuck her tongue out behind Mum's back.

"I'll be fine, Mum," she grumbled as Mum went off to find her other mitten.

"I know you can't wait to see Bailey, love, but you don't have a nice spotty fur coat like he does, so you need to put your hat and scarf on," Mum said firmly.

Eventually Emily was allowed to go,
and she raced next door to meet Granny
and Bailey. Bailey was still in Granny's
little garden, and he started dashing
about happily when he saw Emily.
Granny called him and he bounded over,
skidding to a halt at her feet and gazing
up at her adoringly.

"Aw, he loves you, Granny!" Emily said delightedly as she bent down to stroke his back. Bailey wasn't nearly as shy this morning. It looked like the Battersea lady was right – he was settling in brilliantly!

Off to the Park!

When Granny saw that Emily had brought the rackets, she went to the shed to dig out some tennis balls. Standing in the shed she bounced the balls out of the door to Emily as she found them – and Bailey thought it was the best game ever! As the balls came out he raced Emily to try and catch them first, and when she caught one he scrambled at her legs, woofing at her excitedly until she let him have it.

"He wasn't that interested in any of his dog toys," said Granny, shaking her head. "Typical! I buy him lots of lovely things and all he wants is an old tennis ball!"

It really was chilly when they eventually set off for the park, and Emily's breath came out in a foggy cloud. She was suddenly grateful that she had her mittens to keep her fingers from freezing off!

As they walked into the

park Bailey started whimpering and
pulling on his lead.

"Whatever's the matter, Bailey?"
Granny asked him as she stroked his
nose. Just then a large golden retriever
bounded past, and Bailey shrank down
even further, trying to hide himself
behind Granny's legs.

"He's a bit scared of the other dogs, Emily," Granny told her. "Let's walk round with him slowly until he gets used to it all."

After a while Bailey started getting more and more curious about things. First he slowed down to sniff at some flower beds, and then he wandered over to explore an interesting smell near a

tree. Eventually he was pulling on the lead all the time as he dashed from one edge of the path to the other.

When he was distracted by a lady passing by with a buggy, Granny bent down and slipped his lead off. Emily giggled as Bailey trotted alongside them without noticing, and then laughed out loud when he dashed off and then came to a sudden halt – looking really surprised that he could get so far away!

When they got to the duck pond, Granny and Emily had a rest on one of the benches. Bailey kept on exploring, but he came back over to them every few minutes to check they were still there. Emily and Granny usually loved to sit and watch the ducks – but watching Bailey was much funnier. He had a drink from the pond, went in and out of every bush and had lots of fun yapping at the ducks – until he went up to sniff one that was asleep on the bank and it turned on him with a loud, indignant QUACK!

Bailey shot back
to Granny and
Emily and hid
under the bench.

"Oh, poor
Bailey!" said
Emily, picking him
up for a cuddle.
"Come on, we won't let the big bad duck
get you! Let's go and play with the ball."

They went off and found a nice patch
of grass, and started passing the ball

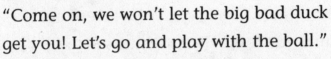

around. Granny threw it
gently to Emily and
Emily tossed it
back – but
almost before it
left her hand
there was a blur
of fur and Bailey

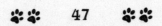

was suddenly on the other side of
Granny, the tennis ball held firmly in his
mouth. He dropped the ball between his
front paws and crouched over it, his tail
wagging excitedly. "*Woof!*" he barked, as
if to say, *This is my ball, paws off!*

Emily and Granny looked at each
other and burst out laughing. "I think
we're going to have to find another game
to play, Em," Granny said, "one that
doesn't involve tennis balls!"

New Friends

Walking in the park was really different now they had Bailey with them. As they passed the other dog walkers, the dogs came over to sniff hello to Bailey, and Granny stopped to talk to their owners.

The first dog they passed was a black standard poodle. He was so much bigger than Bailey that the little Dalmatian could walk underneath his belly!

"I thought poodles were *little* dogs?"
Emily said as she stroked his lovely
woolly fur.

"You're thinking of miniature
poodles," said the lady owner, "this is
how big the standard poodles
are. You couldn't fit one of
these in your handbag!"

Bailey was very shy at first and he lay down every time the poodle went towards him. The poodle didn't seem to mind, he kept going over to Bailey, giving him a nudge, and then trotting away with his tongue out as if to say, *Chase me*!

After a few attempts, Bailey shyly started following him, and eventually they were running around together all over the place.

While the dogs rushed about, Emily looked back at Granny and the poodle lady. Emily's teacher had said that people looked often like their dogs, and actually, she noticed, the poodle lady's hat looked very black and woolly – sort of like her poodle's fur!

Granny had better grow some spots so she looks more like Bailey! Emily thought with a grin.

Eventually Bailey
and the poodle
hurtled back
over to Emily.
Right in front of
her the poodle
sniffed Bailey so
hard that the
little dog fell over!

Emily expected Bailey to be scared –
but he just scrabbled onto his feet and
pounced on the bigger dog. It looked like
Bailey had discovered
that playing
with other
dogs
could be
an awful
lot of fun.

When Granny had finished talking to the lady with the poodle, Emily and Bailey took off at a run. All the leaves had fallen off the trees and were lying in piles just waiting to be jumped in, so they ran in and out of them, and even picked up some to shower over Granny.

"Goodness gracious!" Granny said as the leaves stuck in her hair, "we're all going to need our coats brushed after this!"

Emily's nose and cheeks were bright red by the time they headed back to Granny's cottage. "I've got just the thing to warm us up!" Granny announced. "Hot chocolate!"

"*Woof*!" Bailey agreed.

"Not for you, my lamb," chuckled Granny, giving him a stroke, "but I'm sure we can rustle up a dog biscuit or two. You must be hungry after all that running about. I got tired just watching you!"

When they got in, Emily took off
Bailey's lead as Granny bustled around in
the kitchen. Granny came out with a tray
laden with hot chocolate and home-made
honey cake for her and Emily, and dog
biscuits and water for Bailey. She lit the
fire and sat down in her favourite chair
with a sigh.

Emily sat down happily next to Bailey
and started munching her cake, stroking
Bailey behind the ears with her free
hand. It had been the most brilliant day.

Everything was so much fun now that Bailey was here – Granny was always jolly, but with Bailey around she was happier than ever!

As Emily looked at the little puppy, he gave an enormous snore – he was fast asleep!

"Look, Granny!" Emily whispered, turning round to look at her grandma – but to her surprise Granny had her eyes closed too. Emily got up quietly and pulled a blanket over Granny. She gave her a kiss on her soft cheek and pecked Bailey on the top of his head before she tiptoed out of the door.

As she left, she looked back on the sleepy pair and hugged herself. She was so pleased they'd picked Bailey – he and Granny were quite similar after all!

More Spots
Than Usual!

The next day, Granny asked Emily and Mum to look after Bailey while she went to her painting class.

"Can we take a DVD round, Mum?" Emily asked. "Maybe we can show Bailey *101 Dalmatians!*"

"Oh yes, I'm sure he'd like that," Mum laughed. "I'm pretty sure Granny's pleased that we only got her one, though!"

But when Emily and Mum went next door with the DVD, Granny met them with a frown on her face.

"I think I'm going to have to take Bailey with me to my class," she said worriedly. "He had a bit of a scare this morning when the postman put the post through the door, and he's been sticking to my side like glue all afternoon."

Sure enough, Bailey was poking his head out from behind Granny's skirt.

"Besides, I think it'll be good for him to be in a group of people," Granny said, stroking Bailey's ears. "Maybe then he'll learn that we're not going to hurt him, and he won't be so scared of the postman, will you, you silly little thing?"

"OK," said Emily in a small voice, looking down at her shoes.

"Why don't you go too, Em?" Mum suggested. "Then you can look after Bailey and Granny can do her painting. And you can do some painting too, if you want."

"Oh yes, that
sounds like a good
idea," Granny
agreed, smiling.
"We're supposed
to be doing a
rather nice still
life of a fruit bowl
– and I wouldn't
want to miss out."

A fruit bowl? Emily thought, *why would
you want to paint fruit when you could paint
something really beautiful?*

"I already know what I'm going to
paint, Granny," Emily said excitedly.
"The most beautiful thing of all – Bailey!"

"OK, love," said Granny. "I'm not sure
whether you'll get him to be a *still* life,
though!"

Mum dropped them off at the painting class, which was in the same school hall that Emily came to for Brownies. Granny had a lovely time showing Bailey to her friends as they each came round to give him a stroke. Then they all went and sat in their places, in a circle around a raised platform with a table and a bowl of fruit on it.

Granny gave Emily a pad of paper and a set of paints.

"I think I'm only going to need black and white if I'm painting Bailey!" Emily joked.

"Oh, I think you'll need more than that," Granny replied. "Look how lovely and blue his eyes are, and how red his tongue is!"

Bailey was lying under Granny's chair, so Emily spread out on the floor next to him and tried to concentrate on sketching his face. But it was so hard! When 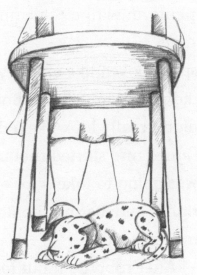 she drew his nose it looked like an elephant's trunk, and all his Dalmatian

spots looked like extra eyes. Her drawing didn't look much like Bailey – in fact it didn't really look like a dog at all. Emily sighed and started rubbing out again. It was going to take a lot of work to get this right – maybe she should have tried the fruit instead!

After rubbing it out for what felt like the hundredth time, Emily rested her head on her arm while she looked at Bailey.

It was so warm and quiet
in the hall that Emily
started feeling quite
sleepy . . .

Bailey had been sitting quietly under
Granny's chair for a while, and, just like
in the park, his curiosity was getting the
better of him. While the ladies were
chatting away overhead, Bailey started
slowly creeping out, and edged towards
Emily. Emily was fast asleep. Bailey gave
her a little nudge with his nose, but she

didn't move, so he looked at her paints. He put his nose down to sniff one – and got red paint all over his nose!

Bailey didn't like the feeling of the wet paint at all, and rubbed his nose with his paw. Now he had a red paw too! He whined and went over to sit next to Emily. He nudged her, but when he got no response he curled up next to her – lying right on top of her wet painting . . .

Emily woke up when she felt a lick on her face. She looked round, confused. She couldn't believe she'd fallen asleep. And she was meant to be watching Bailey. She looked for the little dog and . . . shrieked! Bailey was covered in splotches of paint!

Granny looked round when she heard Emily yell, and gasped when she saw her paint-splattered puppy.

"Emily!" she laughed, "when you said you were going to paint Bailey, this wasn't quite what I thought you meant!"

The Unwelcome Visitor

It took a while to get Bailey cleaned up. He wasn't that keen on having a bath, and both Emily and her mum had to hold the squirming, slippery little pup as Granny washed the paint off his fur. Emily's mum said that Bailey didn't need to watch *101 Dalmatians* – he could get in enough trouble on his own, without getting any ideas from Pongo and his friends.

"Besides," Granny said, as she washed one of Bailey's ears, "if he's scared of the postman, imagine how petrified he'd be of Cruella de Vil!"

Despite her nap at the school hall, Emily was yawning by the time she and Mum said goodnight to Granny and Bailey and went next door to bed.

It felt like she'd just dropped off to sleep when Emily was woken up by a noise. Sleepily rubbing her eyes she wandered over to the window to look outside.

What she saw made her wide awake – there was someone in Granny's garden! Emily strained her eyes to try and make out the shape in the darkness – there was definitely someone there, and they were creeping towards Granny's back door!

"MUM!" Emily yelled in a frightened voice. "*MUM!*"

When there was no reply, Emily tore across the hall to her mum's room, stumbling into things in the dark. Running over to the bed, Emily started shaking her mum, half crying.

"Mum, Mum, wake up – there's a burglar in Granny's garden!"

"OK," said Mum, sleepily, "it was probably a dream, love."

"MUM!" said Emily loudly. "There's a BURGLAR in Granny's garden! Come and see!

Mum pulled herself out of bed and went to look through Emily's window.

"What is that?" Emily's mum murmured when she saw the shape by the house. Then suddenly the man turned on a torch and they could see him crouching by the door, trying to force it open with a crowbar.

Mum gasped. "Oh my word, it *is* a burglar – Emily, stay here and watch to make sure he doesn't go in. I've got to call the police!"

"But what about Granny?" Emily wailed.

"The police will come and look after Granny, don't worry," Mum said, as she sped downstairs. Soon Emily could hear

 her talking quietly on the phone, but she couldn't tear her eyes away from the window. Just then the burglar did something with the crowbar and the door burst open.

"Mum!" Emily called in alarm – but before the man could get through the door, Bailey came hurtling out, throwing himself at the burglar and barking like crazy!

The man tried to push past the frantic little dog, but Bailey blocked his way, growling and looking really menacing.

As Emily watched, terrified, a light came on in Granny's house, and Emily saw Granny's concerned face at the window, looking down to see what the commotion was all about. Emily sobbed with worry as Mum shouted up the stairs.

"I'm going round to check Granny's OK – I'll lock the front door behind me, so stay there."

Just then they heard sirens in the distance. The police were nearly here.

The man must have heard them too, because he gave up trying to get into the house and rushed to the end of the garden. *Oh, no,* thought Emily, *is he going to get away?*

Brave Bailey

The burglar ran to the garden fence and started climbing up it, but Bailey dashed towards him and leaped up, grabbing the edge of his trousers in his teeth. The burglar kicked out at him and moved his leg to try and shake Bailey off, but the brave little puppy clung on. The burglar swung his leg further – and lost his balance. He fell heavily to the ground –

just as three burly policemen burst in to
the garden!

The policemen rushed over and
grabbed him, and Bailey shot back into
the house. Emily and Mum
dashed over to check
on Granny, and
found her in the
kitchen, clutching a
frying pan! Bailey
was by her legs
again, but instead
of cowering
behind them he
was standing in
front protectively.

One of the policemen drove the
burglar off to the police station and the
other two came and took a report from
Emily and Mum, while Granny made
them all hot chocolate.

"Bailey was such a hero!" said Mum, making a big fuss of him. "Who'd have thought that this shy little puppy could be so brave!"

"He's certainly helped us out," said one of the policemen. "There have been a lot of burglaries in this area recently, and we're very pleased to have caught the person responsible."

"Yes," added the other policeman, patting Bailey's head,

"If Bailey ever wants to be a police dog we could do with him on the Force!"

"I think I'll keep him as my guard dog," said Granny as she sipped her hot chocolate. Emily noticed that her hand was a bit shaky and gave her a squeeze.

"Don't worry, Mrs Taylor," one of the policemen reassured her. "Put a good strong bolt on the back door and it'll be perfectly secure again. Besides, I don't think anyone's going to be getting past this little fellow!"

"*Woof*!" agreed Bailey. Granny laughed and scooped him up into her lap for a cuddle.

She got some of the whipped cream from
the top of her hot chocolate on her finger
and held it out for Bailey to lick. "There
you go, you brave puppy,"
she said, "you deserve
a treat after the way
you looked after
me tonight."

Once the policemen had left, Emily's mum herded Emily, Granny and Bailey into Granny's cosy lounge and gathered them in for a big hug on the sofa.

Bailey took pride of place in the
middle, and gave an enormous puppy
yawn, which set everyone else off
yawning as well.

"I certainly am lucky," said Granny, looking at them all. "Not only do I have a wonderful daughter and granddaughter, but they found me the bravest puppy ever as well!"

She stroked Bailey's soft head and the little puppy gave a snore. Emily's eyes were shutting too, and Granny smiled as she tucked her in. "Goodnight everyone." she whispered. "Sweet dreams!"

Read on for lots more . . .

❖ ❖ ❖ ❖

Battersea Dogs & Cats Home

Battersea Dogs & Cats Home is a charity that aims never to turn away a dog or cat in need of our help. We reunite lost dogs and cats with their owners; when we can't do this, we care for them until new homes can be found for them; and we educate the public about responsible pet ownership. Every year the Home takes in around 12,000 dogs and cats. In addition to the site in southwest London, the Home also has two other centres based at Old Windsor, Berkshire and Brands Hatch, Kent.

The original site in Holloway

History

The Temporary Home for Lost and
Starving Dogs was originally opened in a
stable yard in Holloway in 1860 by Mary
Tealby after she found a starving puppy
in the street. There was no one to look
after him, so she took him home and
nursed him back to health. Mary was so
worried about the other dogs wandering
the streets that she opened The
Temporary Home for Lost and Starving
Dogs. The Home was established to help
to look after them all and to help to find
them new homes.

Sadly Mary Tealby died in 1865, aged
sixty-four, and little more is known about
her but her good work was continued. In
1871, the Home moved to its present site

in Battersea, and was renamed The Dogs' Home Battersea.

Some important dates for the Home:
1883 – Battersea started taking in cats.

1914 – 100 sledge dogs are housed at the Hackbridge site, in preparation for Ernest Shackleton's second Antarctic expedition.

1956 – Queen Elizabeth II became patron of the Home.

2004 – Red the Lurcher's night-time antics become world famous when he is caught on camera regularly escaping his kennel and liberating his canine chums for midnight feasting.

2007 – The BBC broadcast *Animal Rescue Live* live from the Home for three weeks from mid-July to early August.

Amy Watson

Amy Watson has been working at Battersea Dogs & Cats Home for six years and has been the Home's Education Officer for three. Amy's role means that she organizes all of the school visits to the Home for children aged sixteen and under, and regularly visits schools around

Battersea's three sites to teach children how to behave and stay safe around dogs and cats and to understand the importance of responsible dog and cat ownership. She also regularly features on the Battersea website – www.battersea.org.uk – giving tips and advice on how to train your dog or cat under the Amy's Answers section.

On most school visits Amy can take a dog with her, so she is normally accompanied by her beautiful ex-Battersea dog Hattie. Hattie has been living with Amy for just over a year and really enjoys her visits to meet new children and help Amy with her work.

What the process is for re-homing a dog or a cat

When a lost dog or cat arrives, Battersea's Lost Dogs & Cats team works hard to try to find the animal's owners. If, after seven days they cannot reunite them, the search for a new home can begin.

The Home works hard to find all the lost and unwanted dogs and cats caring, permanent new homes.

Dogs and cats have their own characters and so staff at the Home will spend time with every dog and cat getting to know them. This helps decide the type of home the dog or cat needs.

There are five stages of the rehoming process at Battersea Dogs & Cats Home. Battersea's re-homing team wants to find you the perfect pet and sometimes this can take a while, so please be patient while we search for your new friend!

1 Application

2 Interview

3 Home visit

4 Searching for a pet

5 Leaving with your new pet

Have a look at our website:
http://www.battersea.org.uk/dogs/ rehoming/index.html for more details!

Did you know? questions about dogs and cats

• Puppies do not open their eyes until they are about two weeks old.

• According to the *Guinness Book of Records*, the smallest living dog is a long- haired Chihuahua called Danka Kordak from Slovakia, who is 13.8 cm tall and 18.8 cm long.

• Dalmatians, with all those cute black spots, are actually born white.

• The greyhound is the fastest dog on earth. They can run up to 45 miles per hour.

• The first living creature sent into space was a female dog named Laika.

• Cats spend 15% of their day grooming themselves and a massive 70% of their day sleeping.

• Cats see six times better than we do in the dark.

• A cat's tail helps it to balance when it is on the move – especially when the cat is jumping.

• The cat, giraffe and camel are the only animals that walk by moving both their left feet, then both their right feet, when walking.

Dos and Don'ts of looking after dogs and cats

Dogs dos and don'ts

DO

- Be gentle and quiet around dogs at all times – treat them how you would like to be treated.
- Have respect for dogs.

DON'T

- Sneak up on a dog – you could scare them.
- Tease a dog – it's not fair.
- Stare at a dog – dogs can find this scary.
- Disturb a dog who is sleeping or eating.

- Assume a dog wants to play. Just like you, sometimes they may want to be left alone.
- Approach a dog who is without an owner as you won't know if the dog is friendly or not.

Cats dos and don'ts

DO
- Be gentle and quiet around cats at all times.
- Have respect for cats.
- Let a cat approach you in her own time.

DON'T
- Stare at a cat as she can find this intimidating.
- Tease a cat – it's not fair.

- Disturb a sleeping or eating cat – she may not want attention or to play
- Assume a cat will always want to play. Like you, sometimes they want to be left alone.

Here is a delicious recipe for you to follow.

Remember to ask an adult to help you.

Cheddar Cheese Dog Cookies

You will need:

225g grated Cheddar cheese
(use at room temperature)

115g margarine

1 egg

1 clove of garlic (crushed)

170g wholewheat flour

30g wheatgerm,

1 teaspoon of salt

30ml milk

Preheat the oven to 375 degrees F/
190 degrees C/ gas mark 5.

Cream the cheese and margarine together, when smooth add the egg and garlic and mix well. Add the flour, wheatgerm and salt, mix well until a dough forms.

Add the milk and mix again.

Chill the mixture for one hour in the fridge.

Roll the dough onto a floured surface

until it is about 4 cm thick.

Use cookie cutters to cut out shapes.

Bake on an ungreased baking tray for 15–18 minutes.

Cool to room temperature and store in an airtight container in the fridge.

Some fun pet-themed puzzles!

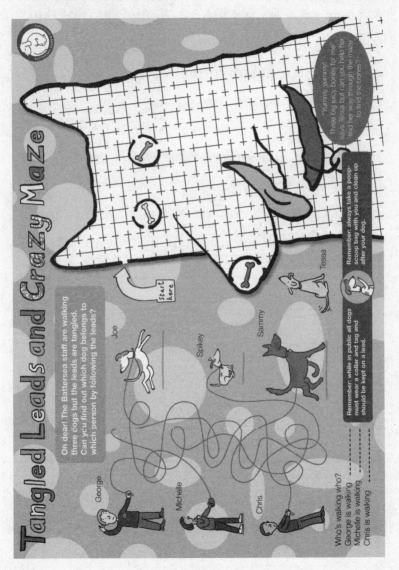

Tangled Leads and Crazy Maze

Oh dear! The Battersea staff are walking three dogs but the leads are tangled. Can you find out which dog belongs to which person by following the leads?

"Yummy yummy! Three big juicy bones for me" says Tessa but can't you help her find her way through the maze to find the bones?

Remember: always take a poop-scoop bag with you and clean up after your dog.

Remember: while in public all dogs must wear a collar and tag and should be kept on a lead.

start here

Joe

Spikey

Sammy

Tessa

George

Michelle

Chris

Who's walking who?
George is walking --------------
Michelle is walking --------------
Chris is walking --------------

109

What to think about before getting a dog!

Here is a list of things that you need to think about before getting a dog. See if you can find them in the word search and while you look, think why they might be so important. Only look for words written in blue. They can be written backwards, diagonally, forwards, up and down so look carefully and GOOD LUCK!

SIZE
MALE OR FEMALE
AGE
COAT TYPE
COST
BEHAVIOUR
BASIC TRAINING
HOUSE TRAINING
TIME ALONE
GOOD WITH: PETS, CHILDREN,
STRANGERS, DOGS
HOW: ENERGETIC, CUDDLY,
STRONG WILLED, INDEPENDENT

Remember: when training a dog, reward works better than punishment.

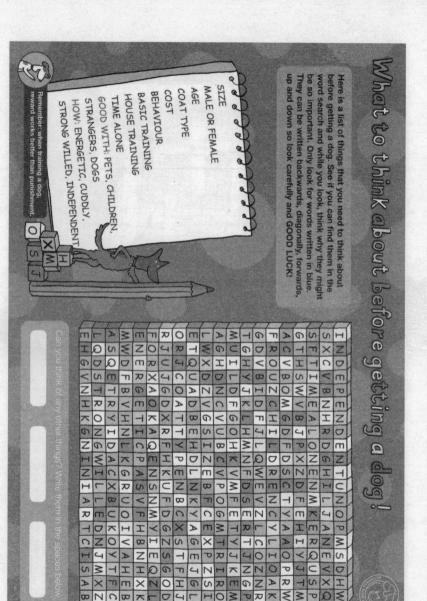

Can you think of any other things? Write them in the spaces below.

Dog Breeds Crossword

Across

2. A breed used as police dogs and sometimes called an Alsatian (6,8)
5. A dog that is a mixture of breeds (7)
6. A breed commonly used as guide dogs for the blind. (8)
9. Smallest breed of dog (9)
11. A brown/liver and white breed often referred to as a bird dogs. (8,7)
14. A French breed with very curly hair, traditionally used as a gun dog. (6)
15. A small black and tan terrier that was used to catch rats (6)
16. A small white terrier from Scotland (4)
17. A small breed with short legs and a long back, sometimes called a sausage dog. (9)
18. The dog often used as the symbol of Great Britain. (7)

Down

1. A spotted dog from a Disney film that needs lots of walking as a pet. (6)
3. A breed associated with a brand of paint. (3,7,8)
4. This breed is used to herd sheep and needs lots of activity such as agility if kept as a pet. (6,6)
7. Eddie from the programme Frasier is one of these. (4,7)
8. A breed associated with a brand of sherry. (6,6)
10. Scooby Doo was one of these very large dogs. (5,4)
12. These dogs are used for racing but also make good pets. (9)
13. Smaller version of 'Lassie' dog. (7)

Help!
All is trying to count the dogs but some of them keep running about. How many can you count?

Remember: all dogs need exercise in order to keep them fit and healthy and to give mental stimulation.

111

There are lots of fun things on the
website including an online quiz, e-cards,
colouring sheets and more recipes for
making dog and cat treats.

www.battersea.org.uk